Gareth And Lynette

Alfred Lord Tennyson

© 2023 Culturea Editions
Texte et illustration de couverture : © domaine public
Edition : Culturea (Hérault, 34)
Contact : infos@culturea.fr
Retrouvez notre catalogue sur http://culturea.fr
Imprimé en Allemagne par Books on Demand
Design typographique : Derek Murphy
Layout : Reedsy (https://reedsy.com/)
ISBN : 9791041817320
Dépôt légal : Juin 2023
Tous droits réservés pour tous pays

Gareth And Lynette

The last tall son of Lot and Bellicent,
And tallest, Gareth, in a showerful spring
Stared at the spate. A slender-shafted Pine
Lost footing, fell, and so was whirled away.
'How he went down,' said Gareth, 'as a false knight
Or evil king before my lance if lance
Were mine to use--O senseless cataract,
Bearing all down in thy precipitancy--
And yet thou art but swollen with cold snows
And mine is living blood: thou dost His will,
The Maker's, and not knowest, and I that know,
Have strength and wit, in my good mother's hall
Linger with vacillating obedience,
Prisoned, and kept and coaxed and whistled to--
Since the good mother holds me still a child!
Good mother is bad mother unto me!
A worse were better; yet no worse would I.
Heaven yield her for it, but in me put force
To weary her ears with one continuous prayer,
Until she let me fly discaged to sweep
In ever-highering eagle-circles up
To the great Sun of Glory, and thence swoop
Down upon all things base, and dash them dead,
A knight of Arthur, working out his will,
To cleanse the world. Why, Gawain, when he came
With Modred hither in the summertime,
Asked me to tilt with him, the proven knight.
Modred for want of worthier was the judge.
Then I so shook him in the saddle, he said,
"Thou hast half prevailed against me," said so--he--
Though Modred biting his thin lips was mute,
For he is alway sullen: what care I?'

And Gareth went, and hovering round her chair
Asked, 'Mother, though ye count me still the child,
Sweet mother, do ye love the child?' She laughed,
'Thou art but a wild-goose to question it.'
'Then, mother, an ye love the child,' he said,

'Being a goose and rather tame than wild,
Hear the child's story.' 'Yea, my well-beloved,
An 'twere but of the goose and golden eggs.'

And Gareth answered her with kindling eyes,
'Nay, nay, good mother, but this egg of mine
Was finer gold than any goose can lay;
For this an Eagle, a royal Eagle, laid
Almost beyond eye-reach, on such a palm
As glitters gilded in thy Book of Hours.
And there was ever haunting round the palm
A lusty youth, but poor, who often saw
The splendour sparkling from aloft, and thought
"An I could climb and lay my hand upon it,
Then were I wealthier than a leash of kings."
But ever when he reached a hand to climb,
One, that had loved him from his childhood, caught
And stayed him, "Climb not lest thou break thy neck,
I charge thee by my love," and so the boy,
Sweet mother, neither clomb, nor brake his neck,
But brake his very heart in pining for it,
And past away.'

To whom the mother said,
'True love, sweet son, had risked himself and climbed,
And handed down the golden treasure to him.'

And Gareth answered her with kindling eyes,
'Gold?' said I gold?--ay then, why he, or she,
Or whosoe'er it was, or half the world
Had ventured--HAD the thing I spake of been
Mere gold--but this was all of that true steel,
Whereof they forged the brand Excalibur,
And lightnings played about it in the storm,
And all the little fowl were flurried at it,
And there were cries and clashings in the nest,
That sent him from his senses: let me go.'

Then Bellicent bemoaned herself and said,
'Hast thou no pity upon my loneliness?

Lo, where thy father Lot beside the hearth
Lies like a log, and all but smouldered out!
For ever since when traitor to the King
He fought against him in the Barons' war,
And Arthur gave him back his territory,
His age hath slowly droopt, and now lies there
A yet-warm corpse, and yet unburiable,
No more; nor sees, nor hears, nor speaks, nor knows.
And both thy brethren are in Arthur's hall,
Albeit neither loved with that full love
I feel for thee, nor worthy such a love:
Stay therefore thou; red berries charm the bird,
And thee, mine innocent, the jousts, the wars,
Who never knewest finger-ache, nor pang
Of wrenched or broken limb--an often chance
In those brain-stunning shocks, and tourney-falls,
Frights to my heart; but stay: follow the deer
By these tall firs and our fast-falling burns;
So make thy manhood mightier day by day;
Sweet is the chase: and I will seek thee out
Some comfortable bride and fair, to grace
Thy climbing life, and cherish my prone year,
Till falling into Lot's forgetfulness
I know not thee, myself, nor anything.
Stay, my best son! ye are yet more boy than man.'

Then Gareth, 'An ye hold me yet for child,
Hear yet once more the story of the child.
For, mother, there was once a King, like ours.
The prince his heir, when tall and marriageable,
Asked for a bride; and thereupon the King
Set two before him. One was fair, strong, armed--
But to be won by force--and many men
Desired her; one good lack, no man desired.
And these were the conditions of the King:
That save he won the first by force, he needs
Must wed that other, whom no man desired,
A red-faced bride who knew herself so vile,
That evermore she longed to hide herself,
Nor fronted man or woman, eye to eye--

Yea--some she cleaved to, but they died of her.
And one--they called her Fame; and one,--O Mother,
How can ye keep me tethered to you--Shame.
Man am I grown, a man's work must I do.
Follow the deer? follow the Christ, the King,
Live pure, speak true, right wrong, follow the King--
Else, wherefore born?'

To whom the mother said
'Sweet son, for there be many who deem him not,
Or will not deem him, wholly proven King--
Albeit in mine own heart I knew him King,
When I was frequent with him in my youth,
And heard him Kingly speak, and doubted him
No more than he, himself; but felt him mine,
Of closest kin to me: yet--wilt thou leave
Thine easeful biding here, and risk thine all,
Life, limbs, for one that is not proven King?
Stay, till the cloud that settles round his birth
Hath lifted but a little. Stay, sweet son.'

And Gareth answered quickly, 'Not an hour,
So that ye yield me--I will walk through fire,
Mother, to gain it--your full leave to go.
Not proven, who swept the dust of ruined Rome
From off the threshold of the realm, and crushed
The Idolaters, and made the people free?
Who should be King save him who makes us free?'

So when the Queen, who long had sought in vain
To break him from the intent to which he grew,
Found her son's will unwaveringly one,
She answered craftily, 'Will ye walk through fire?
Who walks through fire will hardly heed the smoke.
Ay, go then, an ye must: only one proof,
Before thou ask the King to make thee knight,
Of thine obedience and thy love to me,
Thy mother,--I demand.

And Gareth cried,

'A hard one, or a hundred, so I go.
Nay--quick! the proof to prove me to the quick!'

But slowly spake the mother looking at him,
'Prince, thou shalt go disguised to Arthur's hall,
And hire thyself to serve for meats and drinks
Among the scullions and the kitchen-knaves,
And those that hand the dish across the bar.
Nor shalt thou tell thy name to anyone.
And thou shalt serve a twelvemonth and a day.'

For so the Queen believed that when her son
Beheld his only way to glory lead
Low down through villain kitchen-vassalage,
Her own true Gareth was too princely-proud
To pass thereby; so should he rest with her,
Closed in her castle from the sound of arms.

Silent awhile was Gareth, then replied,
'The thrall in person may be free in soul,
And I shall see the jousts. Thy son am I,
And since thou art my mother, must obey.
I therefore yield me freely to thy will;
For hence will I, disguised, and hire myself
To serve with scullions and with kitchen-knaves;
Nor tell my name to any--no, not the King.'

Gareth awhile lingered. The mother's eye
Full of the wistful fear that he would go,
And turning toward him wheresoe'er he turned,
Perplext his outward purpose, till an hour,
When wakened by the wind which with full voice
Swept bellowing through the darkness on to dawn,
He rose, and out of slumber calling two
That still had tended on him from his birth,
Before the wakeful mother heard him, went.

The three were clad like tillers of the soil.
Southward they set their faces. The birds made
Melody on branch, and melody in mid air.

The damp hill-slopes were quickened into green,
And the live green had kindled into flowers,
For it was past the time of Easterday.

So, when their feet were planted on the plain
That broadened toward the base of Camelot,
Far off they saw the silver-misty morn
Rolling her smoke about the Royal mount,
That rose between the forest and the field.
At times the summit of the high city flashed;
At times the spires and turrets half-way down
Pricked through the mist; at times the great gate shone
Only, that opened on the field below:
Anon, the whole fair city had disappeared.

Then those who went with Gareth were amazed,
One crying, 'Let us go no further, lord.
Here is a city of Enchanters, built
By fairy Kings.' The second echoed him,
'Lord, we have heard from our wise man at home
To Northward, that this King is not the King,
But only changeling out of Fairyland,
Who drave the heathen hence by sorcery
And Merlin's glamour.' Then the first again,
'Lord, there is no such city anywhere,
But all a vision.'

Gareth answered them
With laughter, swearing he had glamour enow
In his own blood, his princedom, youth and hopes,
To plunge old Merlin in the Arabian sea;
So pushed them all unwilling toward the gate.
And there was no gate like it under heaven.
For barefoot on the keystone, which was lined
And rippled like an ever-fleeting wave,
The Lady of the Lake stood: all her dress
Wept from her sides as water flowing away;
But like the cross her great and goodly arms
Stretched under the cornice and upheld:
And drops of water fell from either hand;

And down from one a sword was hung, from one
A censer, either worn with wind and storm;
And o'er her breast floated the sacred fish;
And in the space to left of her, and right,
Were Arthur's wars in weird devices done,
New things and old co-twisted, as if Time
Were nothing, so inveterately, that men
Were giddy gazing there; and over all
High on the top were those three Queens, the friends
Of Arthur, who should help him at his need.

Then those with Gareth for so long a space
Stared at the figures, that at last it seemed
The dragon-boughts and elvish emblemings
Began to move, seethe, twine and curl: they called
To Gareth, 'Lord, the gateway is alive.'

And Gareth likewise on them fixt his eyes
So long, that even to him they seemed to move.
Out of the city a blast of music pealed.
Back from the gate started the three, to whom
From out thereunder came an ancient man,
Long-bearded, saying, 'Who be ye, my sons?'

Then Gareth, 'We be tillers of the soil,
Who leaving share in furrow come to see
The glories of our King: but these, my men,
(Your city moved so weirdly in the mist)
Doubt if the King be King at all, or come
From Fairyland; and whether this be built
By magic, and by fairy Kings and Queens;
Or whether there be any city at all,
Or all a vision: and this music now
Hath scared them both, but tell thou these the truth.'

Then that old Seer made answer playing on him
And saying, 'Son, I have seen the good ship sail
Keel upward, and mast downward, in the heavens,
And solid turrets topsy-turvy in air:
And here is truth; but an it please thee not,

Take thou the truth as thou hast told it me.
For truly as thou sayest, a Fairy King
And Fairy Queens have built the city, son;
They came from out a sacred mountain-cleft
Toward the sunrise, each with harp in hand,
And built it to the music of their harps.
And, as thou sayest, it is enchanted, son,
For there is nothing in it as it seems
Saving the King; though some there be that hold
The King a shadow, and the city real:
Yet take thou heed of him, for, so thou pass
Beneath this archway, then wilt thou become
A thrall to his enchantments, for the King
Will bind thee by such vows, as is a shame
A man should not be bound by, yet the which
No man can keep; but, so thou dread to swear,
Pass not beneath this gateway, but abide
Without, among the cattle of the field.
For an ye heard a music, like enow
They are building still, seeing the city is built
To music, therefore never built at all,
And therefore built for ever.'

Gareth spake
Angered, 'Old master, reverence thine own beard
That looks as white as utter truth, and seems
Wellnigh as long as thou art statured tall!
Why mockest thou the stranger that hath been
To thee fair-spoken?'

But the Seer replied,
'Know ye not then the Riddling of the Bards?
"Confusion, and illusion, and relation,
Elusion, and occasion, and evasion"?
I mock thee not but as thou mockest me,
And all that see thee, for thou art not who
Thou seemest, but I know thee who thou art.
And now thou goest up to mock the King,
Who cannot brook the shadow of any lie.'

Unmockingly the mocker ending here
Turned to the right, and past along the plain;
Whom Gareth looking after said, 'My men,
Our one white lie sits like a little ghost
Here on the threshold of our enterprise.
Let love be blamed for it, not she, nor I:
Well, we will make amends.'

With all good cheer
He spake and laughed, then entered with his twain
Camelot, a city of shadowy palaces
And stately, rich in emblem and the work
Of ancient kings who did their days in stone;
Which Merlin's hand, the Mage at Arthur's court,
Knowing all arts, had touched, and everywhere
At Arthur's ordinance, tipt with lessening peak
And pinnacle, and had made it spire to heaven.
And ever and anon a knight would pass
Outward, or inward to the hall: his arms
Clashed; and the sound was good to Gareth's ear.
And out of bower and casement shyly glanced
Eyes of pure women, wholesome stars of love;
And all about a healthful people stept
As in the presence of a gracious king.

Then into hall Gareth ascending heard
A voice, the voice of Arthur, and beheld
Far over heads in that long-vaulted hall
The splendour of the presence of the King
Throned, and delivering doom--and looked no more--
But felt his young heart hammering in his ears,
And thought, 'For this half-shadow of a lie
The truthful King will doom me when I speak.'
Yet pressing on, though all in fear to find
Sir Gawain or Sir Modred, saw nor one
Nor other, but in all the listening eyes
Of those tall knights, that ranged about the throne,
Clear honour shining like the dewy star
Of dawn, and faith in their great King, with pure
Affection, and the light of victory,

And glory gained, and evermore to gain.
Then came a widow crying to the King,
'A boon, Sir King! Thy father, Uther, reft
From my dead lord a field with violence:
For howsoe'er at first he proffered gold,
Yet, for the field was pleasant in our eyes,
We yielded not; and then he reft us of it
Perforce, and left us neither gold nor field.'

Said Arthur, 'Whether would ye? gold or field?'
To whom the woman weeping, 'Nay, my lord,
The field was pleasant in my husband's eye.'

And Arthur, 'Have thy pleasant field again,
And thrice the gold for Uther's use thereof,
According to the years. No boon is here,
But justice, so thy say be proven true.
Accursed, who from the wrongs his father did
Would shape himself a right!'

And while she past,
Came yet another widow crying to him,
'A boon, Sir King! Thine enemy, King, am I.
With thine own hand thou slewest my dear lord,
A knight of Uther in the Barons' war,
When Lot and many another rose and fought
Against thee, saying thou wert basely born.
I held with these, and loathe to ask thee aught.
Yet lo! my husband's brother had my son
Thralled in his castle, and hath starved him dead;
And standeth seized of that inheritance
Which thou that slewest the sire hast left the son.
So though I scarce can ask it thee for hate,
Grant me some knight to do the battle for me,
Kill the foul thief, and wreak me for my son.'

Then strode a good knight forward, crying to him,
'A boon, Sir King! I am her kinsman, I.
Give me to right her wrong, and slay the man.'

Then came Sir Kay, the seneschal, and cried,
'A boon, Sir King! even that thou grant her none,
This railer, that hath mocked thee in full hall--
None; or the wholesome boon of gyve and gag.'

But Arthur, 'We sit King, to help the wronged
Through all our realm. The woman loves her lord.
Peace to thee, woman, with thy loves and hates!
The kings of old had doomed thee to the flames,
Aurelius Emrys would have scourged thee dead,
And Uther slit thy tongue: but get thee hence--
Lest that rough humour of the kings of old
Return upon me! Thou that art her kin,
Go likewise; lay him low and slay him not,
But bring him here, that I may judge the right,
According to the justice of the King:
Then, be he guilty, by that deathless King
Who lived and died for men, the man shall die.'

Then came in hall the messenger of Mark,
A name of evil savour in the land,
The Cornish king. In either hand he bore
What dazzled all, and shone far-off as shines
A field of charlock in the sudden sun
Between two showers, a cloth of palest gold,
Which down he laid before the throne, and knelt,
Delivering, that his lord, the vassal king,
Was even upon his way to Camelot;
For having heard that Arthur of his grace
Had made his goodly cousin, Tristram, knight,
And, for himself was of the greater state,
Being a king, he trusted his liege-lord
Would yield him this large honour all the more;
So prayed him well to accept this cloth of gold,
In token of true heart and felty.

Then Arthur cried to rend the cloth, to rend
In pieces, and so cast it on the hearth.
An oak-tree smouldered there. 'The goodly knight!
What! shall the shield of Mark stand among these?'

For, midway down the side of that long hall
A stately pile,--whereof along the front,
Some blazoned, some but carven, and some blank,
There ran a treble range of stony shields,--
Rose, and high-arching overbrowed the hearth.
And under every shield a knight was named:
For this was Arthur's custom in his hall;
When some good knight had done one noble deed,
His arms were carven only; but if twain
His arms were blazoned also; but if none,
The shield was blank and bare without a sign
Saving the name beneath; and Gareth saw
The shield of Gawain blazoned rich and bright,
And Modred's blank as death; and Arthur cried
To rend the cloth and cast it on the hearth.

'More like are we to reave him of his crown
Than make him knight because men call him king.
The kings we found, ye know we stayed their hands
From war among themselves, but left them kings;
Of whom were any bounteous, merciful,
Truth-speaking, brave, good livers, them we enrolled
Among us, and they sit within our hall.
But as Mark hath tarnished the great name of king,
As Mark would sully the low state of churl:
And, seeing he hath sent us cloth of gold,
Return, and meet, and hold him from our eyes,
Lest we should lap him up in cloth of lead,
Silenced for ever--craven--a man of plots,
Craft, poisonous counsels, wayside ambushings--
No fault of thine: let Kay the seneschal
Look to thy wants, and send thee satisfied--
Accursed, who strikes nor lets the hand be seen!'

And many another suppliant crying came
With noise of ravage wrought by beast and man,
And evermore a knight would ride away.

Last, Gareth leaning both hands heavily
Down on the shoulders of the twain, his men,

Approached between them toward the King, and asked,
'A boon, Sir King (his voice was all ashamed),
For see ye not how weak and hungerworn
I seem--leaning on these? grant me to serve
For meat and drink among thy kitchen-knaves
A twelvemonth and a day, nor seek my name.
Hereafter I will fight.'

To him the King,
'A goodly youth and worth a goodlier boon!
But so thou wilt no goodlier, then must Kay,
The master of the meats and drinks, be thine.'

He rose and past; then Kay, a man of mien
Wan-sallow as the plant that feels itself
Root-bitten by white lichen,

'Lo ye now!
This fellow hath broken from some Abbey, where,
God wot, he had not beef and brewis enow,
However that might chance! but an he work,
Like any pigeon will I cram his crop,
And sleeker shall he shine than any hog.'

Then Lancelot standing near, 'Sir Seneschal,
Sleuth-hound thou knowest, and gray, and all the
hounds;
A horse thou knowest, a man thou dost not know:
Broad brows and fair, a fluent hair and fine,
High nose, a nostril large and fine, and hands
Large, fair and fine!--Some young lad's mystery--
But, or from sheepcot or king's hall, the boy
Is noble-natured. Treat him with all grace,
Lest he should come to shame thy judging of him.'

Then Kay, 'What murmurest thou of mystery?
Think ye this fellow will poison the King's dish?
Nay, for he spake too fool-like: mystery!
Tut, an the lad were noble, he had asked
For horse and armour: fair and fine, forsooth!

Sir Fine-face, Sir Fair-hands? but see thou to it
That thine own fineness, Lancelot, some fine day
Undo thee not--and leave my man to me.'

So Gareth all for glory underwent
The sooty yoke of kitchen-vassalage;
Ate with young lads his portion by the door,
And couched at night with grimy kitchen-knaves.
And Lancelot ever spake him pleasantly,
But Kay the seneschal, who loved him not,
Would hustle and harry him, and labour him
Beyond his comrade of the hearth, and set
To turn the broach, draw water, or hew wood,
Or grosser tasks; and Gareth bowed himself
With all obedience to the King, and wrought
All kind of service with a noble ease
That graced the lowliest act in doing it.
And when the thralls had talk among themselves,
And one would praise the love that linkt the King
And Lancelot--how the King had saved his life
In battle twice, and Lancelot once the King's--
For Lancelot was the first in Tournament,
But Arthur mightiest on the battle-field--
Gareth was glad. Or if some other told,
How once the wandering forester at dawn,
Far over the blue tarns and hazy seas,
On Caer-Eryri's highest found the King,
A naked babe, of whom the Prophet spake,
'He passes to the Isle Avilion,
He passes and is healed and cannot die'--
Gareth was glad. But if their talk were foul,
Then would he whistle rapid as any lark,
Or carol some old roundelay, and so loud
That first they mocked, but, after, reverenced him.
Or Gareth telling some prodigious tale
Of knights, who sliced a red life-bubbling way
Through twenty folds of twisted dragon, held
All in a gap-mouthed circle his good mates
Lying or sitting round him, idle hands,
Charmed; till Sir Kay, the seneschal, would come

Blustering upon them, like a sudden wind
Among dead leaves, and drive them all apart.
Or when the thralls had sport among themselves,
So there were any trial of mastery,
He, by two yards in casting bar or stone
Was counted best; and if there chanced a joust,
So that Sir Kay nodded him leave to go,
Would hurry thither, and when he saw the knights
Clash like the coming and retiring wave,
And the spear spring, and good horse reel, the boy
Was half beyond himself for ecstasy.

So for a month he wrought among the thralls;
But in the weeks that followed, the good Queen,
Repentant of the word she made him swear,
And saddening in her childless castle, sent,
Between the in-crescent and de-crescent moon,
Arms for her son, and loosed him from his vow.

This, Gareth hearing from a squire of Lot
With whom he used to play at tourney once,
When both were children, and in lonely haunts
Would scratch a ragged oval on the sand,
And each at either dash from either end--
Shame never made girl redder than Gareth joy.
He laughed; he sprang. 'Out of the smoke, at once
I leap from Satan's foot to Peter's knee--
These news be mine, none other's--nay, the King's--
Descend into the city:' whereon he sought
The King alone, and found, and told him all.

'I have staggered thy strong Gawain in a tilt
For pastime; yea, he said it: joust can I.
Make me thy knight--in secret! let my name
Be hidden, and give me the first quest, I spring
Like flame from ashes.'

Here the King's calm eye
Fell on, and checked, and made him flush, and bow
Lowly, to kiss his hand, who answered him,

'Son, the good mother let me know thee here,
And sent her wish that I would yield thee thine.
Make thee my knight? my knights are sworn to vows
Of utter hardihood, utter gentleness,
And, loving, utter faithfulness in love,
And uttermost obedience to the King.'

Then Gareth, lightly springing from his knees,
'My King, for hardihood I can promise thee.
For uttermost obedience make demand
Of whom ye gave me to, the Seneschal,
No mellow master of the meats and drinks!
And as for love, God wot, I love not yet,
But love I shall, God willing.'

And the King
'Make thee my knight in secret? yea, but he,
Our noblest brother, and our truest man,
And one with me in all, he needs must know.'

'Let Lancelot know, my King, let Lancelot know,
Thy noblest and thy truest!'

And the King--
'But wherefore would ye men should wonder at you?
Nay, rather for the sake of me, their King,
And the deed's sake my knighthood do the deed,
Than to be noised of.'

Merrily Gareth asked,
'Have I not earned my cake in baking of it?
Let be my name until I make my name!
My deeds will speak: it is but for a day.'
So with a kindly hand on Gareth's arm
Smiled the great King, and half-unwillingly
Loving his lusty youthhood yielded to him.
Then, after summoning Lancelot privily,
'I have given him the first quest: he is not proven.
Look therefore when he calls for this in hall,
Thou get to horse and follow him far away.

Cover the lions on thy shield, and see
Far as thou mayest, he be nor ta'en nor slain.'

Then that same day there past into the hall
A damsel of high lineage, and a brow
May-blossom, and a cheek of apple-blossom,
Hawk-eyes; and lightly was her slender nose
Tip-tilted like the petal of a flower;
She into hall past with her page and cried,

'O King, for thou hast driven the foe without,
See to the foe within! bridge, ford, beset
By bandits, everyone that owns a tower
The Lord for half a league. Why sit ye there?
Rest would I not, Sir King, an I were king,
Till even the lonest hold were all as free
From cursd bloodshed, as thine altar-cloth
From that best blood it is a sin to spill.'

'Comfort thyself,' said Arthur. 'I nor mine
Rest: so my knighthood keep the vows they swore,
The wastest moorland of our realm shall be
Safe, damsel, as the centre of this hall.
What is thy name? thy need?'

'My name?' she said--
'Lynette my name; noble; my need, a knight
To combat for my sister, Lyonors,
A lady of high lineage, of great lands,
And comely, yea, and comelier than myself.
She lives in Castle Perilous: a river
Runs in three loops about her living-place;
And o'er it are three passings, and three knights
Defend the passings, brethren, and a fourth
And of that four the mightiest, holds her stayed
In her own castle, and so besieges her
To break her will, and make her wed with him:
And but delays his purport till thou send
To do the battle with him, thy chief man
Sir Lancelot whom he trusts to overthrow,

Then wed, with glory: but she will not wed
Save whom she loveth, or a holy life.
Now therefore have I come for Lancelot.'

Then Arthur mindful of Sir Gareth asked,
'Damsel, ye know this Order lives to crush
All wrongers of the Realm. But say, these four,
Who be they? What the fashion of the men?'

'They be of foolish fashion, O Sir King,
The fashion of that old knight-errantry
Who ride abroad, and do but what they will;
Courteous or bestial from the moment, such
As have nor law nor king; and three of these
Proud in their fantasy call themselves the Day,
Morning-Star, and Noon-Sun, and Evening-Star,
Being strong fools; and never a whit more wise
The fourth, who alway rideth armed in black,
A huge man-beast of boundless savagery.
He names himself the Night and oftener Death,
And wears a helmet mounted with a skull,
And bears a skeleton figured on his arms,
To show that who may slay or scape the three,
Slain by himself, shall enter endless night.
And all these four be fools, but mighty men,
And therefore am I come for Lancelot.'

Hereat Sir Gareth called from where he rose,
A head with kindling eyes above the throng,
'A boon, Sir King--this quest!' then--for he marked
Kay near him groaning like a wounded bull--
'Yea, King, thou knowest thy kitchen-knave am I,
And mighty through thy meats and drinks am I,
And I can topple over a hundred such.
Thy promise, King,' and Arthur glancing at him,
Brought down a momentary brow. 'Rough, sudden,
And pardonable, worthy to be knight--
Go therefore,' and all hearers were amazed.

But on the damsel's forehead shame, pride, wrath

Slew the May-white: she lifted either arm,
'Fie on thee, King! I asked for thy chief knight,
And thou hast given me but a kitchen-knave.'
Then ere a man in hall could stay her, turned,
Fled down the lane of access to the King,
Took horse, descended the slope street, and past
The weird white gate, and paused without, beside
The field of tourney, murmuring 'kitchen-knave.'

Now two great entries opened from the hall,
At one end one, that gave upon a range
Of level pavement where the King would pace
At sunrise, gazing over plain and wood;
And down from this a lordly stairway sloped
Till lost in blowing trees and tops of towers;
And out by this main doorway past the King.
But one was counter to the hearth, and rose
High that the highest-crested helm could ride
Therethrough nor graze: and by this entry fled
The damsel in her wrath, and on to this
Sir Gareth strode, and saw without the door
King Arthur's gift, the worth of half a town,
A warhorse of the best, and near it stood
The two that out of north had followed him:
This bare a maiden shield, a casque; that held
The horse, the spear; whereat Sir Gareth loosed
A cloak that dropt from collar-bone to heel,
A cloth of roughest web, and cast it down,
And from it like a fuel-smothered fire,
That lookt half-dead, brake bright, and flashed as those
Dull-coated things, that making slide apart
Their dusk wing-cases, all beneath there burns
A jewelled harness, ere they pass and fly.
So Gareth ere he parted flashed in arms.
Then as he donned the helm, and took the shield
And mounted horse and graspt a spear, of grain
Storm-strengthened on a windy site, and tipt
With trenchant steel, around him slowly prest
The people, while from out of kitchen came

The thralls in throng, and seeing who had worked
Lustier than any, and whom they could but love,
Mounted in arms, threw up their caps and cried,
'God bless the King, and all his fellowship!'
And on through lanes of shouting Gareth rode
Down the slope street, and past without the gate.

So Gareth past with joy; but as the cur
Pluckt from the cur he fights with, ere his cause
Be cooled by fighting, follows, being named,
His owner, but remembers all, and growls
Remembering, so Sir Kay beside the door
Muttered in scorn of Gareth whom he used
To harry and hustle.

'Bound upon a quest
With horse and arms--the King hath past his time--
My scullion knave! Thralls to your work again,
For an your fire be low ye kindle mine!
Will there be dawn in West and eve in East?
Begone!--my knave!--belike and like enow
Some old head-blow not heeded in his youth
So shook his wits they wander in his prime--
Crazed! How the villain lifted up his voice,
Nor shamed to bawl himself a kitchen-knave.
Tut: he was tame and meek enow with me,
Till peacocked up with Lancelot's noticing.
Well--I will after my loud knave, and learn
Whether he know me for his master yet.
Out of the smoke he came, and so my lance
Hold, by God's grace, he shall into the mire--
Thence, if the King awaken from his craze,
Into the smoke again.'

But Lancelot said,
'Kay, wherefore wilt thou go against the King,
For that did never he whereon ye rail,
But ever meekly served the King in thee?
Abide: take counsel; for this lad is great
And lusty, and knowing both of lance and sword.'

'Tut, tell not me,' said Kay, 'ye are overfine
To mar stout knaves with foolish courtesies:'
Then mounted, on through silent faces rode
Down the slope city, and out beyond the gate.

But by the field of tourney lingering yet
Muttered the damsel, 'Wherefore did the King
Scorn me? for, were Sir Lancelot lackt, at least
He might have yielded to me one of those
Who tilt for lady's love and glory here,
Rather than--O sweet heaven! O fie upon him--
His kitchen-knave.'

To whom Sir Gareth drew
(And there were none but few goodlier than he)
Shining in arms, 'Damsel, the quest is mine.
Lead, and I follow.' She thereat, as one
That smells a foul-fleshed agaric in the holt,
And deems it carrion of some woodland thing,
Or shrew, or weasel, nipt her slender nose
With petulant thumb and finger, shrilling, 'Hence!
Avoid, thou smellest all of kitchen-grease.
And look who comes behind,' for there was Kay.
'Knowest thou not me? thy master? I am Kay.
We lack thee by the hearth.'

And Gareth to him,
'Master no more! too well I know thee, ay--
The most ungentle knight in Arthur's hall.'
'Have at thee then,' said Kay: they shocked, and Kay
Fell shoulder-slipt, and Gareth cried again,
'Lead, and I follow,' and fast away she fled.

But after sod and shingle ceased to fly
Behind her, and the heart of her good horse
Was nigh to burst with violence of the beat,
Perforce she stayed, and overtaken spoke.

'What doest thou, scullion, in my fellowship?
Deem'st thou that I accept thee aught the more

Or love thee better, that by some device
Full cowardly, or by mere unhappiness,
Thou hast overthrown and slain thy master--thou!--
Dish-washer and broach-turner, loon!--to me
Thou smellest all of kitchen as before.'

'Damsel,' Sir Gareth answered gently, 'say
Whate'er ye will, but whatsoe'er ye say,
I leave not till I finish this fair quest,
Or die therefore.'

'Ay, wilt thou finish it?
Sweet lord, how like a noble knight he talks!
The listening rogue hath caught the manner of it.
But, knave, anon thou shalt be met with, knave,
And then by such a one that thou for all
The kitchen brewis that was ever supt
Shalt not once dare to look him in the face.'

'I shall assay,' said Gareth with a smile
That maddened her, and away she flashed again
Down the long avenues of a boundless wood,
And Gareth following was again beknaved.

'Sir Kitchen-knave, I have missed the only way
Where Arthur's men are set along the wood;
The wood is nigh as full of thieves as leaves:
If both be slain, I am rid of thee; but yet,
Sir Scullion, canst thou use that spit of thine?
Fight, an thou canst: I have missed the only way.'

So till the dusk that followed evensong
Rode on the two, reviler and reviled;
Then after one long slope was mounted, saw,
Bowl-shaped, through tops of many thousand pines
A gloomy-gladed hollow slowly sink
To westward--in the deeps whereof a mere,
Round as the red eye of an Eagle-owl,
Under the half-dead sunset glared; and shouts
Ascended, and there brake a servingman

Flying from out of the black wood, and crying,
'They have bound my lord to cast him in the mere.'
Then Gareth, 'Bound am I to right the wronged,
But straitlier bound am I to bide with thee.'
And when the damsel spake contemptuously,
'Lead, and I follow,' Gareth cried again,
'Follow, I lead!' so down among the pines
He plunged; and there, blackshadowed nigh the mere,
And mid-thigh-deep in bulrushes and reed,
Saw six tall men haling a seventh along,
A stone about his neck to drown him in it.
Three with good blows he quieted, but three
Fled through the pines; and Gareth loosed the stone
From off his neck, then in the mere beside
Tumbled it; oilily bubbled up the mere.
Last, Gareth loosed his bonds and on free feet
Set him, a stalwart Baron, Arthur's friend.

'Well that ye came, or else these caitiff rogues
Had wreaked themselves on me; good cause is theirs
To hate me, for my wont hath ever been
To catch my thief, and then like vermin here
Drown him, and with a stone about his neck;
And under this wan water many of them
Lie rotting, but at night let go the stone,
And rise, and flickering in a grimly light
Dance on the mere. Good now, ye have saved a life
Worth somewhat as the cleanser of this wood.
And fain would I reward thee worshipfully.
What guerdon will ye?'
Gareth sharply spake,
'None! for the deed's sake have I done the deed,
In uttermost obedience to the King.
But wilt thou yield this damsel harbourage?'

Whereat the Baron saying, 'I well believe
You be of Arthur's Table,' a light laugh
Broke from Lynette, 'Ay, truly of a truth,
And in a sort, being Arthur's kitchen-knave!--
But deem not I accept thee aught the more,

Scullion, for running sharply with thy spit
Down on a rout of craven foresters.
A thresher with his flail had scattered them.
Nay--for thou smellest of the kitchen still.
But an this lord will yield us harbourage,
Well.'

So she spake. A league beyond the wood,
All in a full-fair manor and a rich,
His towers where that day a feast had been
Held in high hall, and many a viand left,
And many a costly cate, received the three.
And there they placed a peacock in his pride
Before the damsel, and the Baron set
Gareth beside her, but at once she rose.

'Meseems, that here is much discourtesy,
Setting this knave, Lord Baron, at my side.
Hear me--this morn I stood in Arthur's hall,
And prayed the King would grant me Lancelot
To fight the brotherhood of Day and Night--
The last a monster unsubduable
Of any save of him for whom I called--
Suddenly bawls this frontless kitchen-knave,
"The quest is mine; thy kitchen-knave am I,
And mighty through thy meats and drinks am I."
Then Arthur all at once gone mad replies,
"Go therefore," and so gives the quest to him--
Him--here--a villain fitter to stick swine
Than ride abroad redressing women's wrong,
Or sit beside a noble gentlewoman.'

Then half-ashamed and part-amazed, the lord
Now looked at one and now at other, left
The damsel by the peacock in his pride,
And, seating Gareth at another board,
Sat down beside him, ate and then began.

'Friend, whether thou be kitchen-knave, or not,
Or whether it be the maiden's fantasy,

And whether she be mad, or else the King,
Or both or neither, or thyself be mad,
I ask not: but thou strikest a strong stroke,
For strong thou art and goodly therewithal,
And saver of my life; and therefore now,
For here be mighty men to joust with, weigh
Whether thou wilt not with thy damsel back
To crave again Sir Lancelot of the King.
Thy pardon; I but speak for thine avail,
The saver of my life.'

And Gareth said,
'Full pardon, but I follow up the quest,
Despite of Day and Night and Death and Hell.'

So when, next morn, the lord whose life he saved
Had, some brief space, conveyed them on their way
And left them with God-speed, Sir Gareth spake,
'Lead, and I follow.' Haughtily she replied.

'I fly no more: I allow thee for an hour.
Lion and stout have isled together, knave,
In time of flood. Nay, furthermore, methinks
Some ruth is mine for thee. Back wilt thou, fool?
For hard by here is one will overthrow
And slay thee: then will I to court again,
And shame the King for only yielding me
My champion from the ashes of his hearth.'

To whom Sir Gareth answered courteously,
'Say thou thy say, and I will do my deed.
Allow me for mine hour, and thou wilt find
My fortunes all as fair as hers who lay
Among the ashes and wedded the King's son.'

Then to the shore of one of those long loops
Wherethrough the serpent river coiled, they came.
Rough-thicketed were the banks and steep; the stream
Full, narrow; this a bridge of single arc
Took at a leap; and on the further side

Arose a silk pavilion, gay with gold
In streaks and rays, and all Lent-lily in hue,
Save that the dome was purple, and above,
Crimson, a slender banneret fluttering.
And therebefore the lawless warrior paced
Unarmed, and calling, 'Damsel, is this he,
The champion thou hast brought from Arthur's hall?
For whom we let thee pass.' 'Nay, nay,' she said,
'Sir Morning-Star. The King in utter scorn
Of thee and thy much folly hath sent thee here
His kitchen-knave: and look thou to thyself:
See that he fall not on thee suddenly,
And slay thee unarmed: he is not knight but knave.'

Then at his call, 'O daughters of the Dawn,
And servants of the Morning-Star, approach,
Arm me,' from out the silken curtain-folds
Bare-footed and bare-headed three fair girls
In gilt and rosy raiment came: their feet
In dewy grasses glistened; and the hair
All over glanced with dewdrop or with gem
Like sparkles in the stone Avanturine.
These armed him in blue arms, and gave a shield
Blue also, and thereon the morning star.
And Gareth silent gazed upon the knight,
Who stood a moment, ere his horse was brought,
Glorying; and in the stream beneath him, shone
Immingled with Heaven's azure waveringly,
The gay pavilion and the naked feet,
His arms, the rosy raiment, and the star.

Then she that watched him, 'Wherefore stare ye so?
Thou shakest in thy fear: there yet is time:
Flee down the valley before he get to horse.
Who will cry shame? Thou art not knight but knave.'

Said Gareth, 'Damsel, whether knave or knight,
Far liefer had I fight a score of times
Than hear thee so missay me and revile.
Fair words were best for him who fights for thee;

But truly foul are better, for they send
That strength of anger through mine arms, I know
That I shall overthrow him.'

And he that bore
The star, when mounted, cried from o'er the bridge,
'A kitchen-knave, and sent in scorn of me!
Such fight not I, but answer scorn with scorn.
For this were shame to do him further wrong
Than set him on his feet, and take his horse
And arms, and so return him to the King.
Come, therefore, leave thy lady lightly, knave.
Avoid: for it beseemeth not a knave
To ride with such a lady.'

'Dog, thou liest.
I spring from loftier lineage than thine own.'
He spake; and all at fiery speed the two
Shocked on the central bridge, and either spear
Bent but not brake, and either knight at once,
Hurled as a stone from out of a catapult
Beyond his horse's crupper and the bridge,
Fell, as if dead; but quickly rose and drew,
And Gareth lashed so fiercely with his brand
He drave his enemy backward down the bridge,
The damsel crying, 'Well-stricken, kitchen-knave!'
Till Gareth's shield was cloven; but one stroke
Laid him that clove it grovelling on the ground.

Then cried the fallen, 'Take not my life: I yield.'
And Gareth, 'So this damsel ask it of me
Good--I accord it easily as a grace.'
She reddening, 'Insolent scullion: I of thee?
I bound to thee for any favour asked!'
'Then he shall die.' And Gareth there unlaced
His helmet as to slay him, but she shrieked,
'Be not so hardy, scullion, as to slay
One nobler than thyself.' 'Damsel, thy charge
Is an abounding pleasure to me. Knight,
Thy life is thine at her command. Arise

And quickly pass to Arthur's hall, and say
His kitchen-knave hath sent thee. See thou crave
His pardon for thy breaking of his laws.
Myself, when I return, will plead for thee.
Thy shield is mine--farewell; and, damsel, thou,
Lead, and I follow.'

And fast away she fled.
Then when he came upon her, spake, 'Methought,
Knave, when I watched thee striking on the bridge
The savour of thy kitchen came upon me
A little faintlier: but the wind hath changed:
I scent it twenty-fold.' And then she sang,
'"O morning star" (not that tall felon there
Whom thou by sorcery or unhappiness
Or some device, hast foully overthrown),
"O morning star that smilest in the blue,
O star, my morning dream hath proven true,
Smile sweetly, thou! my love hath smiled on me."

'But thou begone, take counsel, and away,
For hard by here is one that guards a ford--
The second brother in their fool's parable--
Will pay thee all thy wages, and to boot.
Care not for shame: thou art not knight but knave.'

To whom Sir Gareth answered, laughingly,
'Parables? Hear a parable of the knave.
When I was kitchen-knave among the rest
Fierce was the hearth, and one of my co-mates
Owned a rough dog, to whom he cast his coat,
"Guard it," and there was none to meddle with it.
And such a coat art thou, and thee the King
Gave me to guard, and such a dog am I,
To worry, and not to flee--and--knight or knave--
The knave that doth thee service as full knight
Is all as good, meseems, as any knight
Toward thy sister's freeing.'

'Ay, Sir Knave!

Ay, knave, because thou strikest as a knight,
Being but knave, I hate thee all the more.'

'Fair damsel, you should worship me the more,
That, being but knave, I throw thine enemies.'

'Ay, ay,' she said, 'but thou shalt meet thy match.'

So when they touched the second river-loop,
Huge on a huge red horse, and all in mail
Burnished to blinding, shone the Noonday Sun
Beyond a raging shallow. As if the flower,
That blows a globe of after arrowlets,
Ten thousand-fold had grown, flashed the fierce shield,
All sun; and Gareth's eyes had flying blots
Before them when he turned from watching him.
He from beyond the roaring shallow roared,
'What doest thou, brother, in my marches here?'
And she athwart the shallow shrilled again,
'Here is a kitchen-knave from Arthur's hall
Hath overthrown thy brother, and hath his arms.'
'Ugh!' cried the Sun, and vizoring up a red
And cipher face of rounded foolishness,
Pushed horse across the foamings of the ford,
Whom Gareth met midstream: no room was there
For lance or tourney-skill: four strokes they struck
With sword, and these were mighty; the new knight
Had fear he might be shamed; but as the Sun
Heaved up a ponderous arm to strike the fifth,
The hoof of his horse slipt in the stream, the stream
Descended, and the Sun was washed away.

Then Gareth laid his lance athwart the ford;
So drew him home; but he that fought no more,
As being all bone-battered on the rock,
Yielded; and Gareth sent him to the King,
'Myself when I return will plead for thee.'
'Lead, and I follow.' Quietly she led.
'Hath not the good wind, damsel, changed again?'
'Nay, not a point: nor art thou victor here.

There lies a ridge of slate across the ford;
His horse thereon stumbled--ay, for I saw it.

'"O Sun" (not this strong fool whom thou, Sir Knave,
Hast overthrown through mere unhappiness),
"O Sun, that wakenest all to bliss or pain,
O moon, that layest all to sleep again,
Shine sweetly: twice my love hath smiled on me."

What knowest thou of lovesong or of love?
Nay, nay, God wot, so thou wert nobly born,
Thou hast a pleasant presence. Yea, perchance,--

'"O dewy flowers that open to the sun,
O dewy flowers that close when day is done,
Blow sweetly: twice my love hath smiled on me."

'What knowest thou of flowers, except, belike,
To garnish meats with? hath not our good King
Who lent me thee, the flower of kitchendom,
A foolish love for flowers? what stick ye round
The pasty? wherewithal deck the boar's head?
Flowers? nay, the boar hath rosemaries and bay.

'"O birds, that warble to the morning sky,
O birds that warble as the day goes by,
Sing sweetly: twice my love hath smiled on me."

'What knowest thou of birds, lark, mavis, merle,
Linnet? what dream ye when they utter forth
May-music growing with the growing light,
Their sweet sun-worship? these be for the snare
(So runs thy fancy) these be for the spit,
Larding and basting. See thou have not now
Larded thy last, except thou turn and fly.
There stands the third fool of their allegory.'

For there beyond a bridge of treble bow,
All in a rose-red from the west, and all
Naked it seemed, and glowing in the broad

Deep-dimpled current underneath, the knight,
That named himself the Star of Evening, stood.

And Gareth, 'Wherefore waits the madman there
Naked in open dayshine?' 'Nay,' she cried,
'Not naked, only wrapt in hardened skins
That fit him like his own; and so ye cleave
His armour off him, these will turn the blade.'

Then the third brother shouted o'er the bridge,
'O brother-star, why shine ye here so low?
Thy ward is higher up: but have ye slain
The damsel's champion?' and the damsel cried,

'No star of thine, but shot from Arthur's heaven
With all disaster unto thine and thee!
For both thy younger brethren have gone down
Before this youth; and so wilt thou, Sir Star;
Art thou not old?'
'Old, damsel, old and hard,
Old, with the might and breath of twenty boys.'
Said Gareth, 'Old, and over-bold in brag!
But that same strength which threw the Morning Star
Can throw the Evening.'

Then that other blew
A hard and deadly note upon the horn.
'Approach and arm me!' With slow steps from out
An old storm-beaten, russet, many-stained
Pavilion, forth a grizzled damsel came,
And armed him in old arms, and brought a helm
With but a drying evergreen for crest,
And gave a shield whereon the Star of Even
Half-tarnished and half-bright, his emblem, shone.
But when it glittered o'er the saddle-bow,
They madly hurled together on the bridge;
And Gareth overthrew him, lighted, drew,
There met him drawn, and overthrew him again,
But up like fire he started: and as oft
As Gareth brought him grovelling on his knees,

So many a time he vaulted up again;
Till Gareth panted hard, and his great heart,
Foredooming all his trouble was in vain,
Laboured within him, for he seemed as one
That all in later, sadder age begins
To war against ill uses of a life,
But these from all his life arise, and cry,
'Thou hast made us lords, and canst not put us down!'
He half despairs; so Gareth seemed to strike
Vainly, the damsel clamouring all the while,
'Well done, knave-knight, well-stricken, O good knight-
knave--
O knave, as noble as any of all the knights--
Shame me not, shame me not. I have prophesied--
Strike, thou art worthy of the Table Round--
His arms are old, he trusts the hardened skin--
Strike--strike--the wind will never change again.'
And Gareth hearing ever stronglier smote,
And hewed great pieces of his armour off him,
But lashed in vain against the hardened skin,
And could not wholly bring him under, more
Than loud Southwesterns, rolling ridge on ridge,
The buoy that rides at sea, and dips and springs
For ever; till at length Sir Gareth's brand
Clashed his, and brake it utterly to the hilt.
'I have thee now;' but forth that other sprang,
And, all unknightlike, writhed his wiry arms
Around him, till he felt, despite his mail,
Strangled, but straining even his uttermost
Cast, and so hurled him headlong o'er the bridge
Down to the river, sink or swim, and cried,
'Lead, and I follow.'

But the damsel said,
'I lead no longer; ride thou at my side;
Thou art the kingliest of all kitchen-knaves.

'"O trefoil, sparkling on the rainy plain,
O rainbow with three colours after rain,
Shine sweetly: thrice my love hath smiled on me."

'Sir,--and, good faith, I fain had added--Knight,
But that I heard thee call thyself a knave,--
Shamed am I that I so rebuked, reviled,
Missaid thee; noble I am; and thought the King
Scorned me and mine; and now thy pardon, friend,
For thou hast ever answered courteously,
And wholly bold thou art, and meek withal
As any of Arthur's best, but, being knave,
Hast mazed my wit: I marvel what thou art.'

'Damsel,' he said, 'you be not all to blame,
Saving that you mistrusted our good King
Would handle scorn, or yield you, asking, one
Not fit to cope your quest. You said your say;
Mine answer was my deed. Good sooth! I hold
He scarce is knight, yea but half-man, nor meet
To fight for gentle damsel, he, who lets
His heart be stirred with any foolish heat
At any gentle damsel's waywardness.
Shamed? care not! thy foul sayings fought for me:
And seeing now thy words are fair, methinks
There rides no knight, not Lancelot, his great self,
Hath force to quell me.'
Nigh upon that hour
When the lone hern forgets his melancholy,
Lets down his other leg, and stretching, dreams
Of goodly supper in the distant pool,
Then turned the noble damsel smiling at him,
And told him of a cavern hard at hand,
Where bread and baken meats and good red wine
Of Southland, which the Lady Lyonors
Had sent her coming champion, waited him.

Anon they past a narrow comb wherein
Where slabs of rock with figures, knights on horse
Sculptured, and deckt in slowly-waning hues.
'Sir Knave, my knight, a hermit once was here,
Whose holy hand hath fashioned on the rock
The war of Time against the soul of man.

And yon four fools have sucked their allegory
From these damp walls, and taken but the form.
Know ye not these?' and Gareth lookt and read--
In letters like to those the vexillary
Hath left crag-carven o'er the streaming Gelt--
'PHOSPHORUS,' then 'MERIDIES'--'HESPERUS'--
'NOX'--'MORS,' beneath five figures, armd men,
Slab after slab, their faces forward all,
And running down the Soul, a Shape that fled
With broken wings, torn raiment and loose hair,
For help and shelter to the hermit's cave.
'Follow the faces, and we find it. Look,
Who comes behind?'

For one--delayed at first
Through helping back the dislocated Kay
To Camelot, then by what thereafter chanced,
The damsel's headlong error through the wood--
Sir Lancelot, having swum the river-loops--
His blue shield-lions covered--softly drew
Behind the twain, and when he saw the star
Gleam, on Sir Gareth's turning to him, cried,
'Stay, felon knight, I avenge me for my friend.'
And Gareth crying pricked against the cry;
But when they closed--in a moment--at one touch
Of that skilled spear, the wonder of the world--
Went sliding down so easily, and fell,
That when he found the grass within his hands
He laughed; the laughter jarred upon Lynette:
Harshly she asked him, 'Shamed and overthrown,
And tumbled back into the kitchen-knave,
Why laugh ye? that ye blew your boast in vain?'
'Nay, noble damsel, but that I, the son
Of old King Lot and good Queen Bellicent,
And victor of the bridges and the ford,
And knight of Arthur, here lie thrown by whom
I know not, all through mere unhappiness--
Device and sorcery and unhappiness--
Out, sword; we are thrown!' And Lancelot answered,
'Prince,

O Gareth--through the mere unhappiness
Of one who came to help thee, not to harm,
Lancelot, and all as glad to find thee whole,
As on the day when Arthur knighted him.'

Then Gareth, 'Thou--Lancelot!--thine the hand
That threw me? An some chance to mar the boast
Thy brethren of thee make--which could not chance--
Had sent thee down before a lesser spear,
Shamed had I been, and sad--O Lancelot--thou!'

Whereat the maiden, petulant, 'Lancelot,
Why came ye not, when called? and wherefore now
Come ye, not called? I gloried in my knave,
Who being still rebuked, would answer still
Courteous as any knight--but now, if knight,
The marvel dies, and leaves me fooled and tricked,
And only wondering wherefore played upon:
And doubtful whether I and mine be scorned.
Where should be truth if not in Arthur's hall,
In Arthur's presence? Knight, knave, prince and fool,
I hate thee and for ever.'

And Lancelot said,
'Blessd be thou, Sir Gareth! knight art thou
To the King's best wish. O damsel, be you wise
To call him shamed, who is but overthrown?
Thrown have I been, nor once, but many a time.
Victor from vanquished issues at the last,
And overthrower from being overthrown.
With sword we have not striven; and thy good horse
And thou are weary; yet not less I felt
Thy manhood through that wearied lance of thine.
Well hast thou done; for all the stream is freed,
And thou hast wreaked his justice on his foes,
And when reviled, hast answered graciously,
And makest merry when overthrown. Prince, Knight
Hail, Knight and Prince, and of our Table Round!'

And then when turning to Lynette he told

The tale of Gareth, petulantly she said,
'Ay well--ay well--for worse than being fooled
Of others, is to fool one's self. A cave,
Sir Lancelot, is hard by, with meats and drinks
And forage for the horse, and flint for fire.
But all about it flies a honeysuckle.
Seek, till we find.' And when they sought and found,
Sir Gareth drank and ate, and all his life
Past into sleep; on whom the maiden gazed.
'Sound sleep be thine! sound cause to sleep hast thou.
Wake lusty! Seem I not as tender to him
As any mother? Ay, but such a one
As all day long hath rated at her child,
And vext his day, but blesses him asleep--
Good lord, how sweetly smells the honeysuckle
In the hushed night, as if the world were one
Of utter peace, and love, and gentleness!
O Lancelot, Lancelot'--and she clapt her hands--
'Full merry am I to find my goodly knave
Is knight and noble. See now, sworn have I,
Else yon black felon had not let me pass,
To bring thee back to do the battle with him.
Thus an thou goest, he will fight thee first;
Who doubts thee victor? so will my knight-knave
Miss the full flower of this accomplishment.'

Said Lancelot, 'Peradventure he, you name,
May know my shield. Let Gareth, an he will,
Change his for mine, and take my charger, fresh,
Not to be spurred, loving the battle as well
As he that rides him.' 'Lancelot-like,' she said,
'Courteous in this, Lord Lancelot, as in all.'

And Gareth, wakening, fiercely clutched the shield;
'Ramp ye lance-splintering lions, on whom all spears
Are rotten sticks! ye seem agape to roar!
Yea, ramp and roar at leaving of your lord!--
Care not, good beasts, so well I care for you.
O noble Lancelot, from my hold on these
Streams virtue--fire--through one that will not shame

Even the shadow of Lancelot under shield.
Hence: let us go.'

Silent the silent field
They traversed. Arthur's harp though summer-wan,
In counter motion to the clouds, allured
The glance of Gareth dreaming on his liege.
A star shot: 'Lo,' said Gareth, 'the foe falls!'
An owl whoopt: 'Hark the victor pealing there!'
Suddenly she that rode upon his left
Clung to the shield that Lancelot lent him, crying,
'Yield, yield him this again: 'tis he must fight:
I curse the tongue that all through yesterday
Reviled thee, and hath wrought on Lancelot now
To lend thee horse and shield: wonders ye have done;
Miracles ye cannot: here is glory enow
In having flung the three: I see thee maimed,
Mangled: I swear thou canst not fling the fourth.'

'And wherefore, damsel? tell me all ye know.
You cannot scare me; nor rough face, or voice,
Brute bulk of limb, or boundless savagery
Appal me from the quest.'

'Nay, Prince,' she cried,
'God wot, I never looked upon the face,
Seeing he never rides abroad by day;
But watched him have I like a phantom pass
Chilling the night: nor have I heard the voice.
Always he made his mouthpiece of a page
Who came and went, and still reported him
As closing in himself the strength of ten,
And when his anger tare him, massacring
Man, woman, lad and girl--yea, the soft babe!
Some hold that he hath swallowed infant flesh,
Monster! O Prince, I went for Lancelot first,
The quest is Lancelot's: give him back the shield.'

Said Gareth laughing, 'An he fight for this,
Belike he wins it as the better man:

Thus--and not else!'

But Lancelot on him urged
All the devisings of their chivalry
When one might meet a mightier than himself;
How best to manage horse, lance, sword and shield,
And so fill up the gap where force might fail
With skill and fineness. Instant were his words.

Then Gareth, 'Here be rules. I know but one--
To dash against mine enemy and win.
Yet have I seen thee victor in the joust,
And seen thy way.' 'Heaven help thee,' sighed Lynette.

Then for a space, and under cloud that grew
To thunder-gloom palling all stars, they rode
In converse till she made her palfrey halt,
Lifted an arm, and softly whispered, 'There.'
And all the three were silent seeing, pitched
Beside the Castle Perilous on flat field,
A huge pavilion like a mountain peak
Sunder the glooming crimson on the marge,
Black, with black banner, and a long black horn
Beside it hanging; which Sir Gareth graspt,
And so, before the two could hinder him,
Sent all his heart and breath through all the horn.
Echoed the walls; a light twinkled; anon
Came lights and lights, and once again he blew;
Whereon were hollow tramplings up and down
And muffled voices heard, and shadows past;
Till high above him, circled with her maids,
The Lady Lyonors at a window stood,
Beautiful among lights, and waving to him
White hands, and courtesy; but when the Prince
Three times had blown--after long hush--at last--
The huge pavilion slowly yielded up,
Through those black foldings, that which housed
therein.
High on a nightblack horse, in nightblack arms,
With white breast-bone, and barren ribs of Death,

And crowned with fleshless laughter--some ten steps--
In the half-light--through the dim dawn--advanced
The monster, and then paused, and spake no word.

But Gareth spake and all indignantly,
'Fool, for thou hast, men say, the strength of ten,
Canst thou not trust the limbs thy God hath given,
But must, to make the terror of thee more,
Trick thyself out in ghastly imageries
Of that which Life hath done with, and the clod,
Less dull than thou, will hide with mantling flowers
As if for pity?' But he spake no word;
Which set the horror higher: a maiden swooned;
The Lady Lyonors wrung her hands and wept,
As doomed to be the bride of Night and Death;
Sir Gareth's head prickled beneath his helm;
And even Sir Lancelot through his warm blood felt
Ice strike, and all that marked him were aghast.

At once Sir Lancelot's charger fiercely neighed,
And Death's dark war-horse bounded forward with him.
Then those that did not blink the terror, saw
That Death was cast to ground, and slowly rose.
But with one stroke Sir Gareth split the skull.
Half fell to right and half to left and lay.
Then with a stronger buffet he clove the helm
As throughly as the skull; and out from this
Issued the bright face of a blooming boy
Fresh as a flower new-born, and crying, 'Knight,
Slay me not: my three brethren bad me do it,
To make a horror all about the house,
And stay the world from Lady Lyonors.
They never dreamed the passes would be past.'
Answered Sir Gareth graciously to one
Not many a moon his younger, 'My fair child,
What madness made thee challenge the chief knight
Of Arthur's hall?' 'Fair Sir, they bad me do it.
They hate the King, and Lancelot, the King's friend,
They hoped to slay him somewhere on the stream,
They never dreamed the passes could be past.'

Then sprang the happier day from underground;
And Lady Lyonors and her house, with dance
And revel and song, made merry over Death,
As being after all their foolish fears
And horrors only proven a blooming boy.
So large mirth lived and Gareth won the quest.

And he that told the tale in older times
Says that Sir Gareth wedded Lyonors,
But he, that told it later, says Lynette.